RHYME TIME

Each d_____
by a p_____
which will be a number.

1. The number after 7 that attracts fish: _____ _____
2. A quintet that leaps into a swimming pool: _____ _____
3. Number before 10 displayed on its own billboard: _____ _____
4. A single male child: _____ _____
5. A pair of cows making noise in unison: _____ _____
6. Enough adult males for a basketball game: _____ _____
7. An additional quartet: _____ _____
8. Release trio from a cage: _____ _____
9. Half a dozen twigs: _____ _____
10. The next minute after 7:10: _____ _____

Illustration: Jerry Zimmerman

Hint on page 46

Answer on page 48

COUNT ON IT

All these letters hold the robot's answer to the computer's question. To find the answer, put all the letters with the same design in the matching section.

HOW MANY
BROTHERS
DO YOU
HAVE?

△ _ _ _ _ _ . □ _ _ _ _ _ ⬠ _ ☆ _ _ _ _ _

○ _ _ _ _ _ - _ _ _ _ _ _ _ .

Look for little clues on each letter to tell you what position it holds in that section.

Illustration: Marc Nadel

Hint on page 46

HALF TIME

You don't have to give us the whole answer as you try to figure out these halves. All the numbers in the questions have something in common. All the answers have just the opposite in common. Can you tell what each common element is?

1. What is half of 6? ___
2. What is half of 2? ___
3. What is half of 10? ___
4. What is half of 14? ___
5. What is half of 22? ___
6. What is half of 18? ___
7. What is half of 26? ___
8. What is half of 34? ___
9. What is half of 42? ___
10. What is half of 50? ___
11. What is half of 66? ___
12. What is half of 30? ___

Hint on page 46

Illustration: Terry Kovalcik

Answer on page 48

DOTS A LOT

*S*olve each problem to find an answer that is a multiple of 3. Then connect the dots in order to find a place with three rings of excitement.

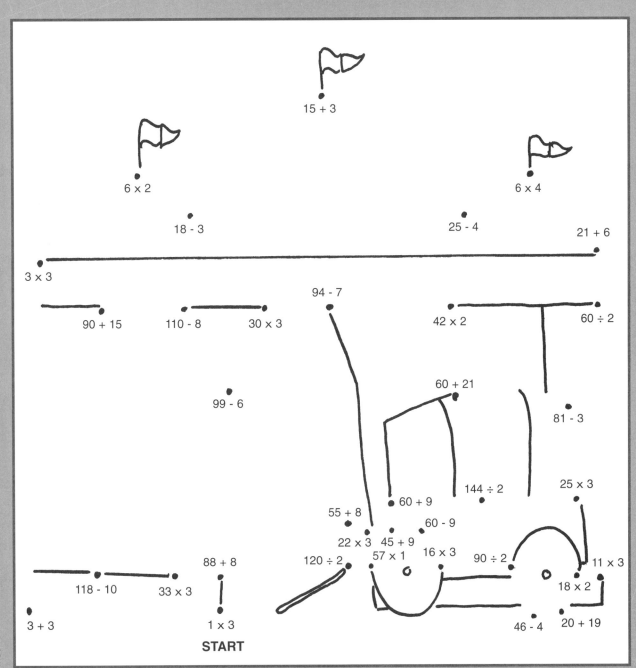

15 + 3

6 × 2

6 × 4

18 - 3

25 - 4

21 + 6

3 × 3

94 - 7

42 × 2

60 ÷ 2

90 + 15

110 - 8

30 × 3

60 + 21

81 - 3

99 - 6

144 ÷ 2

25 × 3

60 + 9

55 + 8

60 - 9

22 × 3

45 + 9

57 × 1

16 × 3

90 ÷ 2

11 × 3

120 ÷ 2

18 × 2

88 + 8

118 - 10

33 × 3

46 - 4

20 + 19

3 + 3

1 × 3

START

Illustration: John Puntar

Answer on page 48

FUNNY GUISE

11 − 2 = __

5 + 2 = __

9 ÷ 3 = __

2 × 3 = __

Answer on page 48

Illustration: Valeri Gorbachev

correct order by numbering
the boxes to show which came
first, then second, and so on?

2 × 1 = __

25 ÷ 5 = __

16 − 8 = __

2 + 2 = __

17 − 16 = __

Hint on page 46

TAKE A MEASURE

Illustration: Barbara Gray

Which is the correct unit of measurement for each item?

Milk—
Gallons or Pounds?

Land—
Acres or Anchors?

Light bulbs—
Weight or Watts?

Ocean—
Fathoms or Furlongs?

HI, DO YOU HAVE THE TIME?

Money—
Quarts or Quarters?

Time—
Seconds or Centimeters?

Apples—
Pounds or Pippins?

Marathon—
Miters or Miles?

DOES THIS RING A BELL?

Answer this, will you? Use the clues to cross off the individual numbers in this grid. When you're done, read the remaining numbers from left to right to discover the year that Alexander Graham Bell, the inventor of the telephone, was born.

Cross off all the digits that
- equal 3 × 3
- equal 3 × 1
- equal 6 × 0
- equal 2 + 2 + 2
- equal 10 - 5
- equal 5 - 3

0	0	5	9	2	0
1	6	3	2	6	5
3	2	0	5	9	3
9	3	8	6	2	9
5	9	0	3	4	6
6	2	9	6	3	7
9	3	2	0	5	3

Illustration: Arnie Ten

HOP TO IT

It's time for the Animal Olympics! Today's event is the long jump. Can you tell which contestants can jump at least as far as the end of the pit? See if you can figure out who the top three medal winners will be.

MATHMANIA

108 INCHES

14 YARDS 1 FOOT

2 YARDS

5 YARDS 1 FOOT

Hint on page 46

Answer on page 48

SHAPE UP

Maria is trying to make some matches. To solve the riddle below, she needs to put the letters shown on the chart into the spaces that have the matching shapes. All spaces with the same shapes get the same letter.

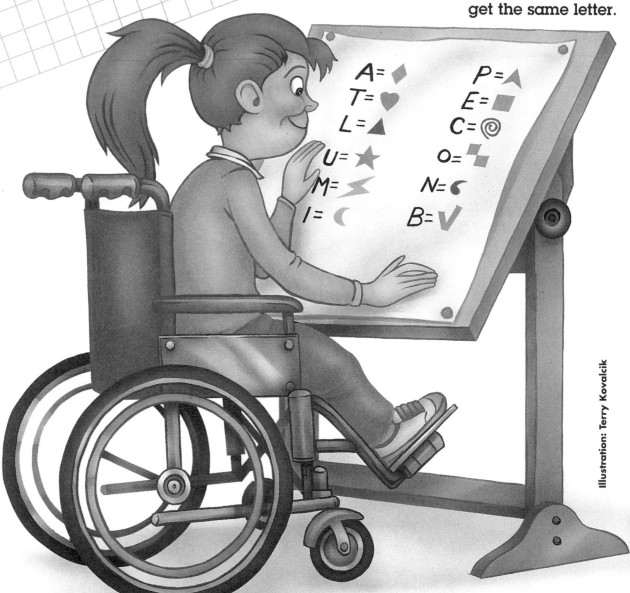

A= ◆
T= ♥
L= ▲
U= ★
M= ⚡
I= ☾

P= ▲
E= ■
C= @
O= ▱
N= ◗
B= ∨

Illustration: Terry Kovalcik

What piece of furniture can be found in all math teachers' kitchens?

Answer on page 49

CUBIC CONFUSION

The shape below can be folded into a cube. The seven cubes above the blank spaces are different views of that cube. Which letter is unseen at the bottom of each cube? When you fill in the blanks with the proper letter, you should find the answer to the riddle.

What tools did the Three Little Pigs use to build their houses?

Illustration: Joe Turowski

SCRAMBLED PICTURE

Copy these mixed-up wedges into the spaces on the next page to unscramble this scene. The letters and

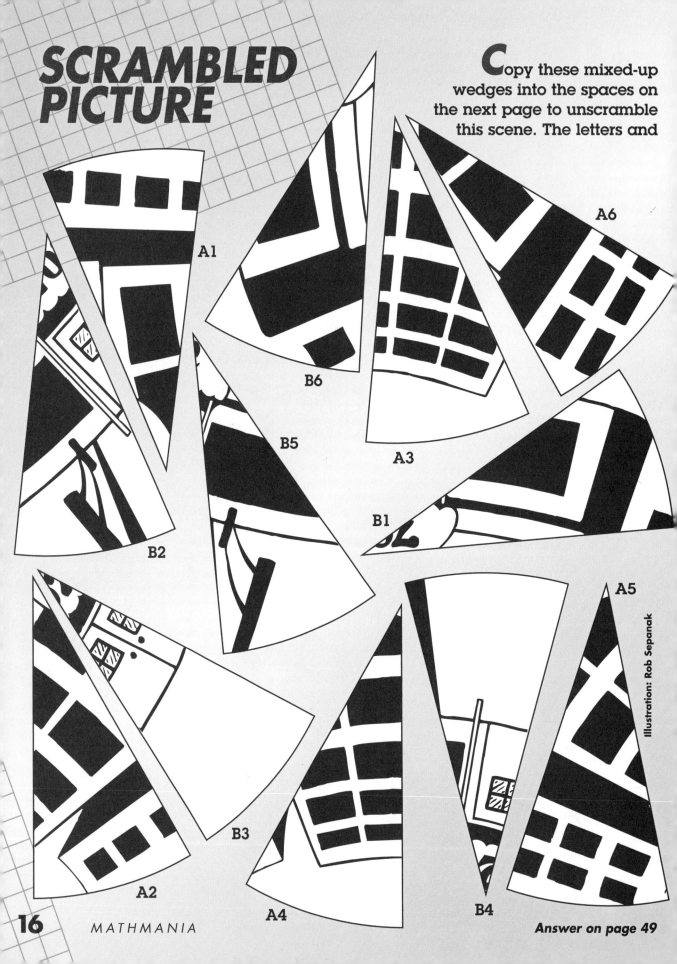

Illustration: Rob Sepanak

Answer on page 49

numbers tell you where
each wedge belongs.
The first one, A3, has been
done for you.

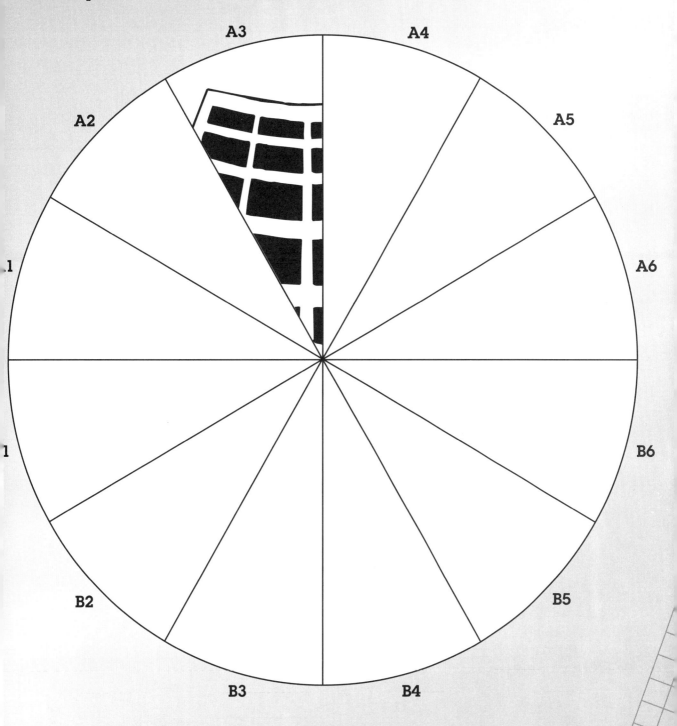

BOX BUILDER

Simone built too many boxes. Can you help her make just four boxes by moving only two sticks to new positions?

Hint on page 46

Illustration: R. Michael Palan

MATH MEMORY

Take 60 seconds to look at this page. Try to remember everything here, especially the numbers. Then turn the page and see if you can answer some questions about this scene without looking back.

$$64 \div 8 =$$
$$5 \times 8 =$$
$$12 \div 2 =$$
$$9 \times 6 =$$

WORDLIES

If you fill in the blanks across to spell six different numbers, you'll have the clues to spell four other numbers from top to bottom.

_ _ U R   _ _ _ _ _

N _ _ E   F _ FTE _ N

SE _ _ N   SI _ TEE _

THRE _

Answer on page 49

MATH MEMORY PART II

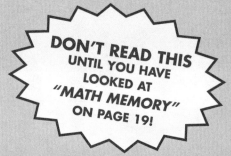

DON'T READ THIS UNTIL YOU HAVE LOOKED AT *"MATH MEMORY"* ON PAGE 19!

1. What type of animal was teaching the class?

2. How many students were in the classroom?

3. What type of animal was sitting closest to the teacher?

4. What time of year was it?

5. How many apples were in the room?

6. How many subtraction problems were on the board?

7. What was the answer to the first problem on the board?

8. What number was on the orangutan's shirt?

Answer on page 49

GRANDMA'S BOXES

Grandma Rita gave her three granddaughters 21 old boxes. Seven of the boxes were filled with jewelry, seven were only half-filled with jewelry, and seven were empty. How can the girls divide all these boxes so that each girl has a fair share of boxes and jewelry?

Hint on page 46

Answer on page 49

DIGIT DOES IT

That super sleuth, Inspector Digit, has done it again. While out for his constitutional, he saw someone snatching some sweets. He stepped in to make a quick

Hint on page 47

arrest. But while he was calling the station, the crook had time to write a message. Can you help Digit decipher the mysterious missive?

$\overline{21}\,\overline{20}\,\overline{19}\,\overline{18}$ $\overline{17}\,\overline{16}\,\overline{15}\,\overline{14}\,\overline{20}\,\overline{13}\,\overline{12}\,\overline{11}\,\overline{18}$ $\overline{21}\,\overline{17}\,\overline{10}\,\overline{17}\,\overline{12}$,
$\overline{17}$ $\overline{12}\,\overline{9}\,\overline{11}\,\overline{8}\,\overline{10}\,\overline{9}\,\overline{12}$ $\overline{12}\,\overline{9}\,\overline{17}\,\overline{15}$ $\overline{7}\,\overline{11}\,\overline{8}\,\overline{2}\,\overline{21}$
$\overline{6}\,\overline{20}$ $\overline{19}$ $\overline{15}\,\overline{7}\,\overline{20}\,\overline{20}\,\overline{12}$ $\overline{13}\,\overline{19}\,\overline{14}\,\overline{20}\,\overline{18}$,
$\overline{6}\,\overline{8}\,\overline{12}$ $\overline{5}\,\overline{11}\,\overline{8}$ $\overline{9}\,\overline{19}\,\overline{21}$ $\overline{12}\,\overline{11}$ $\overline{10}\,\overline{8}\,\overline{4}$
$\overline{8}\,\overline{14}$ $\overline{12}\,\overline{9}\,\overline{20}$ $\overline{7}\,\overline{11}\,\overline{18}\,\overline{3}\,\overline{15}$. $\overline{17}$
$\overline{4}\,\overline{19}\,\overline{16}\,\overline{19}\,\overline{10}\,\overline{20}\,\overline{21}$ $\overline{12}\,\overline{11}$ $\overline{21}\,\overline{18}\,\overline{11}\,\overline{14}$ $\overline{L}\,\overline{Y}$
$\overline{14}\,\overline{17}\,\overline{20}\,\overline{13}\,\overline{20}\,\overline{15}$ $\overline{11}\,\overline{1}$ $\overline{13}\,\overline{19}\,\overline{16}\,\overline{21}\,\overline{5}$ $\overline{13}\,\overline{11}\,\overline{18}\,\overline{16}$
$\overline{6}\,\overline{20}\,\overline{1}\,\overline{11}\,\overline{18}\,\overline{20}$ $\overline{5}\,\overline{11}\,\overline{8}$ $\overline{13}\,\overline{19}\,\overline{4}\,\overline{20}$ $\overline{17}\,\overline{16}$.
$\overline{5}\,\overline{11}\,\overline{8}\,\overline{2}\,\overline{2}$ $\overline{6}\,\overline{20}$ $\overline{19}$ $\overline{15}\,\overline{11}\,\overline{8}\,\overline{18}\,\overline{14}\,\overline{8}\,\overline{15}\,\overline{15}$
$\overline{17}\,\overline{1}$ $\overline{5}\,\overline{11}\,\overline{8}$ $\overline{1}\,\overline{17}\,\overline{16}\,\overline{21}$ $\overline{12}\,\overline{9}\,\overline{20}\,\overline{4}$ $\overline{19}\,\overline{2}\,\overline{2}$
$\overline{6}\,\overline{20}\,\overline{1}\,\overline{11}\,\overline{18}\,\overline{20}$ $\overline{17}$ $\overline{10}\,\overline{20}\,\overline{12}$ $\overline{6}\,\overline{19}\,\overline{13}\,\overline{3}$.
$\overline{20}\,\overline{12}\,\overline{12}\,\overline{19}$ $\overline{13}\,\overline{19}\,\overline{16}\,\overline{21}\,\overline{5}$

Illustration: John Nez

DOT BOXER

This is a dicey problem. Dylan needs to divide this hexagon into nine pieces so that each dot is inside its own rectangle. Each rectangle should be of equal size, and there shouldn't be any space left over.

Hint on page 47

Answer on page 49

PERSONAL NOTES

Hidden in this graph is a short piece from a song titled "A Very Special Person" by Jeff O'Hare. To discover the words, start with *Your*, then move from left to right through the boxes. The words of the song are in the boxes that have 3 as the answer.

_____

_____

3 + 0 Your	32 − 3 along	1 × 2 never	2 + 1 smile	8 ÷ 4 saw
6 − 5 a	5 × 2 big	11 − 3 blue	9 ÷ 3 is	1 + 6 moose
8 ÷ 2 to	4 − 1 like	5 − 3 I	9 − 5 carry	4 + 4 home
2 × 1 hope	3 + 2 my	6 ÷ 3 the	1 + 2 your	3 + 2 swim
0 + 6 leave	1 × 3 mirror.	7 − 5 see	3 + 4 me	2 × 0 running
20 ÷ 2 three	8 + 7 two	4 − 1 It	11 − 9 zero	6 × 3 when
3 × 3 help	6 + 4 the	12 ÷ 4 shows	8 − 4 near	7 − 4 how
9 − 5 baa	3 × 1 very	3 − 1 said	9 − 6 special	10 ÷ 5 chicken
15 ÷ 5 you	0 × 4 wise	5 + 2 we	10 − 2 won't	6 − 3 are.

Answer on page 49

FAIR SHARE

Dan needs to divide this grid into four sections. All sections must be equal in value. Can he count on you for help?

Illustration: Pamela Hodges

Hint on page 47

Answer on page 49

IT'S A SIGN

Illustration: Scott Peck

1. How far is it from where the hikers are to Maxisota?
2. How far is it from Arkandrill to Idono?
3. How far is it from Olowo to Nineasee?
4. How far do you have to go to get from Idono to Old Jersey?
5. Is it farther from Outdiana to Hitasippi or from Pinelahoma to West Dakota?
6. Which two cities are the closest to the signpost?
7. Which two cities are the closest to each other?
8. Which two cities are the farthest away from each other?

ARKANDRILL 300

HITASIPPI 175

Nineasee 650

WEST DAKOTA 900

IDONO 120

PINELAHOMA 80

Maxisota 210

Old Jersey 440

OLOWO 560

OUTDIANA 50

Answer on page 49

MATHMANIA

TRIOS

Each cow scene has something numerical in common with the two others in the same row. Each cow has two horns in the top row across. Look at the other rows of three across, down, or diagonally. Can you find what the trios have in common?

Illustration: Don Robison

Answer on page 50

THE DOG ATE MY HOMEWORK

I t may sound like an excuse, but that's what really happened to Teri's homework. To help her repair it, just figure out what numbers belong in the blank spaces. Then she'll be sure to get an A+.

1.

```
  ⬥⬥35
+ 524⬥
 ─────
  66⬥⬥
- ⬥374
 ─────
  4⬥⬥2
```

2.

```
  7⬥8
+ ⬥1⬥
 ─────
 ⬥107
- 42⬥
 ─────
 ⬥⬥1
```

3.

```
  ⬥1⬥⬥
+ 5⬥13
 ─────
 ⬥677
- 5⬥3⬥
 ─────
 22⬥5
```

Answer on page 50

Hint on page 47

MATHMANIA

29

DOMINANCE

Cheryl says the 18 dominoes on the left can be placed on the board at the right. Meryl is trying to figure out how. She knows that every square will be

Illustration: Joe Turowski

covered, and the dots on the dominoes must match the dots on the board. Each domino will be used once, and every space will be covered. Can you find the answer?

Hint on page 47

TOP VIEWS

Flash Foto has a developing problem. The picture at the top of each strip shows a side view of a group of three-dimensional objects. Can you tell which image in each strip shows a top-down view of these same objects?

Illustration: Jason Thorne

Answer on page 50

COLOR BY NUMBERS

Count the number of sides on each shape below. Then use the key to color in the spaces and find someone corny to hang around with.

KEY	
3 — Yellow	6 — Brown
4 — Blue	7 — Green
5 — Red	8 — Orange

Illustration: Rob Sepanak

NUMBER SEARCH

Hidden in this grid are 41 sayings all having to do with numbers.

1 ON 1	4TH ESTATE
1 SIDED	4TH OF JULY
1 UP	5 AND 10
1 WAY	5 SENSES
2 BITS	6TH SENSE
2 BY 4	7 CONTINENTS
2 FISTED	7 DEADLY SINS
2 POINTS	7 DWARFS
2 STEP	7 HILLS
2 TONE	7 SEAS
3 D	7TH HEAVEN
FIDDLERS 3	7 VIRTUES
3 KITTENS	8 BALL
3 PIGS	8TH NOTE
3 RINGS	8 TRACK
3 TOED SLOTH	9 LADIES
3 WISHES	9 TO 5
4 H	10-4
4 LEAF CLOVER	10 LORDS
4 POSTER	10 PINS
4 SUITS OF CARDS	

Illustration: Beth Griffis Johnson

Look for them across, down,
backward, or diagonally.

```
5 O T 9 H T O L S D E O T 3 N
S 6 4 L E A F C L O V E R E F
E 2 R L S 3 S E U T R I V 7 I
N S 5 A 9 L N 3 10 D N A 5 C D
S N E B 6 O L K 5 G E 2 9 O D
E I S 8 T 3 W I S H E S L N L
S S N 2 B Y 4 T H E S T A T E
I Y E F B P 6 T 6 7 8 E D I R
X L S I O I 7 E H 3 10 P I N S
K D H S V S T N I O P 2 E E 3
C A T T A 10 8 S 2 U F I S N D
A E 6 E 5 Y A W 1 1 5 J G T H
R D S D R A C F O S T I U S 4
T 7 D W A R F S N S D R O L 10
8 T H N O T E 2 1 S I D E D Y
```

North America

Asia

Africa

South America

Australia

Antarctica

PRECISE ICE

A professional skater could go over this figure without crossing over or doubling back along any lines. Can you?

Illustration: Barbara Gray

Answer on page 51

STAR POWER

Answer on page 51

Place the numbers 1 through 15 into these stars. The only problem is, you can't put any number next to a consecutive number, whether it is placed above, below, or diagonally.

Hint on page 47

CLOCK CODE

Check the time to see if you can crack this code. Match the letters on the clocks with the times shown beneath each line.

Illustration: Marc Nadel

What do workers do in a clock factory?

$\overline{}$ $\overline{}$ $\overline{}$ $\overline{}$ $\quad$ $\overline{}$ $\overline{}$ $\overline{}$ $\overline{}$ $\overline{}$
6:15 1:30 3:00 10:30   11:00 1:30 11:30 10:30 9:10

If you make good time, you should find the answers to two riddles.

When is a clock nervous?

— — — — — — — — — — ,
8:30 6:00 10:30 1:00 4:00 6:30 9:10 1:30 6:55 6:55

— — — — — — —
8:30 3:45 3:30 1:00 12:00 3:30 5:05

LONG GON

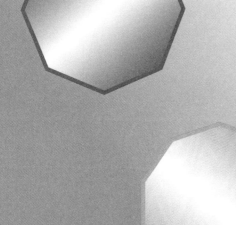

pentagon

hexagon

heptagon

octagon

nonagon

decagon

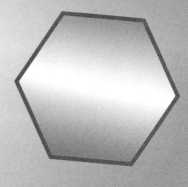

Answer on page 51

MATHMAGIC

This time out, I've got a little something different up my sleeve. I'm going to show you an easy way to remember the 9 times table.

FIRST, write down all the equations from **9** times **0** to **9** times **9** in a column.

9x0=

9x1=

9x2=

9x3=

9x4=

9x5=

9x6=

9x7=

9x8=

9x9=

You probably know that any number times 0 is 0. And you may also know that any number times 1 is that number, which in this case is 9.

But what about the rest?

Count down the column to see how many equations we have left.

Next we say a few magic words — **HYPOTENUSE** and **TANGENT.**

Now count again, this time going up from the bottom.

9×0= 0
9×1= 9
9×2= 1
9×3= 2
9×4= 3
9×5= 4
9×6= 5
9×7= 6
9×8= 7
9×9= 8

Did you discover the trick of the **9** times table?

Illustration: Marc Nadel

ALONG THE RIVER

These intrepid rafters are searching for the longest river rides. To do this, they need to know the world's longest rivers. Look at their list of rivers, then use the clues to match up each river with its

RIVER LENGTH
(in miles)

1,725	1,945
1,979	2,330
2,600	2,600
3,100	3,900
	4,145

RIVERS

Amazon (South America) _____

Danube (Europe) _____

Mekong (Asia) _____

Mississippi (North America) _____

Niger (Africa) _____

Nile (Africa) _____

St. Lawrence (North America) _____

Yangtze (Asia) _____

Yukon (North America) _____

length. Once you've figured out the length of each one, list them in order from the longest to the shortest so that the rafters know which rivers to ride first.

CLUES

The St. Lawrence, Danube, and Yukon Rivers are all under 2,000 miles long.

The Yukon is 34 miles longer than the St. Lawrence.

The Amazon is 800 miles longer than the Yangtze.

The Nile is the longest river.

The Mekong and the Niger are the same length.

Illustration: Scott Peck

Answer on page 51

ANGLE ACTION

Wade in beside this fisherman and see if you can identify the different angles he makes with his rod and line. Match the name of each angle with the proper picture.

ACUTE   OBTUSE
RIGHT   STRAIGHT

Illustration: Jerry Zimmerman

Answer on page 51

Hint on page 47

44

WHY WEIGHT?

Help Hestus figure out the weights of each sphere, cube, and pyramid. Numbers on the weights are shown in pounds.

Answer on page 51

HINTS AND BRIGHT IDEAS

*T*hese hints may help with some of the trickier puzzles.

RHYME TIME (page 3)
You're looking for words that rhyme with certain numbers. The answer to the first one is *eight bait*.

COUNT ON IT (pages 4-5)
Look for design clues to tell you where each letter fits in each word. For example, in the first word, the letter with one triangle is first, the letter with two triangles is second, and so on.

HALF TIME (page 6)
Can't find the common element in each group of numbers? *Even* if you look closely? *Odds* are, you'll figure it out in the end.

FUNNY GUISE (pages 8-9)
Solve the equations beneath each picture. Then put them in order by the value of the answer, starting with the lowest number and working upward.

HOP TO IT (pages 12-13)
The numbers on each shirt represent the distance the animal can jump. There are 12 inches in 1 foot and 3 feet in a yard.

BOX BUILDER (page 18)
Try moving one stick from the top line and one stick from the bottom line.

GRANDMA'S BOXES (page 21)
Jewelry can be moved among the boxes.

DIGIT DOES IT (pages 22-23)

The word *Inspector* appears in the note's greeting. Use the code numbers in this word to help figure out the rest of the message.

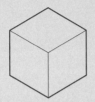

DOT BOXER (page 24)

Think of the hexagon as a three-dimensional object, like a cube. That should help you draw in the first three lines shown here.

FAIR SHARE (page 26)

All pieces must contain the same amount of money. The total of the grid is $324. That means each of the four pieces should hold $81. To start looking for the right shapes, draw a horizontal line between the fourth and fifth rows.

THE DOG ATE MY HOMEWORK (page 29)

The first number in equation 1 is 1435, the first number in equation 2 is 788, and the first number in equation 3 is 2164.

DOMINANCE (pages 30-31)

Some dominoes will go horizontally, while others will fit vertically. The domino marked with one dot in each section goes horizontally in the lower left. If you have your own dominoes, you might use them to help figure this out.

STAR POWER (page 37)

Consecutive numbers cannot be near one another. So for example, a star with a 6 cannot be next to a star with either a 5 or a 7. The number 1 goes in the center, and the number 15 goes in the top left star.

ANGLE ACTION (page 44)

An angle is formed by three points: one at the center and one at either end. A right angle looks like an L, and a straight angle looks like a line. Acute angles are less than 90 degrees, and obtuse angles are over 90 degrees.

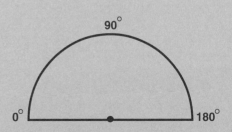

ANSWERS

DOTS A LOT (page 7)

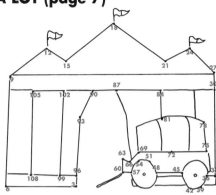

COVER

The scale has two arrows instead of one.
The 7 is a roman numeral.
The 5 is backward.
Numbers 11 and 12 are switched.
Only one banana is in the scale, even though
  the arrows point to 18 and 20.
The 3 is a pyramid of dots.
There are two hash marks between 14 and 15.
The number 1 of the 10 is upside down.
The scale has a second hand like a clock.

RHYME TIME (page 3)

1. Eight bait
2. Five dive
3. Nine sign
4. One son
5. Two moo
6. Ten men
7. Four more
8. Free three
9. Six sticks
10. 7:11

COUNT ON IT (pages 4-5)

How many brothers do you have?
NONE. BUT I HAVE TRAN-SISTORS.

HALF TIME (page 6)

1. 3
2. 1
3. 5
4. 7
5. 11
6. 9
7. 13
8. 17
9. 21
10. 25
11. 33
12. 15

The question numbers are all even.
The answers are all odd.

FUNNY GUISE (pages 8-9)

$17 - 16 = 1$
$2 \times 1 = 2$
$9 \div 3 = 3$
$2 + 2 = 4$
$25 \div 5 = 5$
$2 \times 3 = 6$
$5 + 2 = 7$
$16 - 8 = 8$
$11 - 2 = 9$

Once you number the pictures correctly,
go back and enjoy the story.

TAKE A MEASURE (page 10)

Milk — Gallons
Light bulbs — Watts
Time — Seconds
Apples — Pounds
Land — Acres
Ocean — Fathoms
Money — Quarters
Marathon — Miles

DOES THIS RING A BELL? (page 11)

Alexander Graham Bell was born in 1847.

HOP TO IT (pages 12-13)

Gray squirrel — 6 feet (or 2 yards)
Kangaroo — 43 feet (or 14 yards 1 foot)
Jaguar — 9 feet (or 108 inches)
Cottontail rabbit — 16 feet (or 5 yards 1 foot)
Frog — 10 feet (or 120 inches)
Flea — 1 foot 1 inch (or 13 inches)
Springbok — 11 feet 6 inches
   (or 3 yards $2\frac{1}{2}$ feet)
Horse — 8 feet (or 96 inches)
Giraffe — 2 feet (or 24 inches)

Only the rabbit, kangaroo, frog, and springbok
will reach the end. The kangaroo will take
the gold, the rabbit will take the silver, and
the bronze will go to the springbok.

SHAPE UP (page 14)
What piece of furniture can be found in all math teachers' kitchens?
A MULTIPLICATION TABLE

CUBIC CONFUSION (page 15)
What tools did the Three Little Pigs use to build their houses?
HAM-MERS

SCRAMBLED PICTURE (pages 16-17)

BOX BUILDER (page 18)

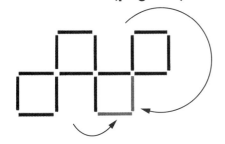

WORDLIES (page 20)
```
      FOUR          S     T
    NINE          FIFTEEN
    SEVEN         SIXTEEN
  THREE
```

MATH MEMORY (page 20)
1. Giraffe
2. Six
3. Panda
4. Winter
5. Two
6. None
7. 8
8. 10

GRANDMA'S BOXES (page 21)
The girls dumped half of each full box into an empty box. That created 21 half-filled boxes, which the girls divided among themselves. Each girl received seven boxes.

DIGIT DOES IT (pages 22-23)
Dear Inspector Digit,
I thought this would be a sweet caper, but you had to gum up the works. I managed to drop 25 pieces of candy corn before you came in. You'll be a sourpuss if you find them all before I get back.   Etta Candy

a–19	m–4
b–6	n–16
c–13	o–11
d–21	p–14
e–20	r–18
f–1	s–15
g–10	t–12
h–9	u–8
i–17	w–7
k–3	y–5
l–2	

DOT BOXER (page 24)

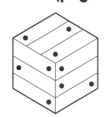

PERSONAL NOTES (page 25)
"Your smile is like your mirror.
It shows how very special you are."

FAIR SHARE (page 26)
Here is our answer. You may have found another.

$5	$5	$25	$1
$5	$25	$10	$10
$10	$5	$5	$10
$1	$10	$10	$25
$20	$10	$5	$5
$5	$1	$10	$10
$15	$5	$20	$20
$5	$5	$1	$25

IT'S A SIGN (page 27)
1. 210 miles
2. 420 miles
3. 90 miles
4. 320 miles
5. Outdiana to Hitasippi—125 miles; Pinelahoma to West Dakota—820 miles
6. Outdiana and Pinelahoma
7. Hitasippi and Maxisota—35 miles
8. West Dakota and Old Jersey—1,340 miles

TRIOS (page 28)

3 flowers 2 flies 4 dark hooves 1 bird

2 horns

1 bell

3 brown patches

1 river

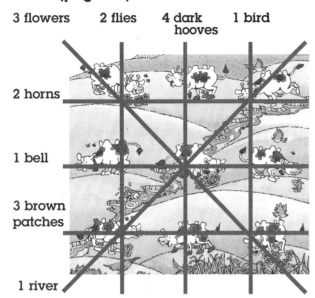

TOP VIEWS (page 32)

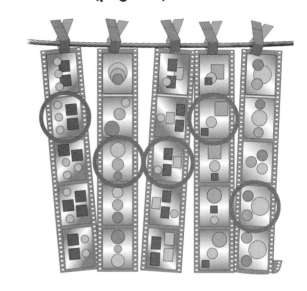

THE DOG ATE MY HOMEWORK (page 29)

1.	2.	3.
1435	788	2164
+5241	+319	+5513
6676	1107	7677
−2374	−426	−5432
4302	681	2245

DOMINANCE (pages 30-31)

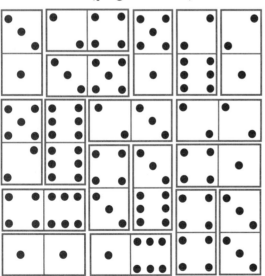

COLOR BY NUMBERS (page 33)

NUMBER SEARCH (pages 34-35)